The INVISIBLE

This book is dedicated to
Isabelle Stevie Lucas – TP

SIMON & SCHUSTER
First published in Great Britain in 2021 by Simon & Schuster UK Ltd
1st Floor, 222 Gray's Inn Road, London WC1X 8HB • Text and illustrations
copyright © 2021 Tom Percival • The right of Tom Percival to be
identified as the author and illustrator of this work has been asserted
by him in accordance with the Copyright, Designs and Patents Act,
1988 • All rights reserved, including the right of reproduction in whole
or in part in any form • A CIP catalogue record for this book is available
from the British Library upon request • ISBN: 978-1-4711-9129-9
(HB) • ISBN: 978-1-4711-9130-5 (PB) • ISBN: 978-1-4711-9131-2 (eBook)
Printed in Great Britain by Bell and Bain Ltd, Glasgow • 10 9 8 7 6 5 4 3 2

The INVISIBLE

TOM PERCIVAL

SIMON & SCHUSTER
London New York Sydney Toronto New Delhi

Isabel pulled on her
favourite jumper.

Ice curled across the inside of the window
and crept up the corner of her bedpost.

It was very beautiful,
and Isabel *always* noticed
beautiful things.

But there was no escaping
the fact that it was also cold.

Very cold.

You see, Isabel's family couldn't afford to have the heating on.

Isabel's family couldn't afford a lot of things.

Things that some people take for granted.

But Isabel tried not to worry about the things she didn't have.

After all, she and her family
had everything that they needed . . .

They had each other.

But one day there just wasn't enough money
to pay the rent and all the bills.

Isabel and her family had to leave their home,
the house which held all their happy memories . . .

and move to the far side of the city.

For the first time ever,
Isabel couldn't find anything
beautiful to cheer herself up.

This part of the city looked exactly
how she felt – cold, sad and lonely.

A family drove past in a shiny car,
but they looked straight through Isabel,

as though she wasn't even there.

None of the other smartly dressed people
seemed to see her either.

Isabel looked down and realised
that she could barely see her own hands . . .

or her feet.

She was fading away.

Before long, Isabel was completely invisible.

She drifted silently down the streets,
as pale and thin as the wind.

And nobody saw her at all.

But now that Isabel was invisible, she noticed something
she hadn't seen before – other invisible people.

LOTS of them.

There was an old lady planting flowers

in empty paint pots.

There was the man who slept on a bench,
feeding the birds in the park.

And there was the boy who had been forced to leave his home in another country, helping to mend someone's bike.

But they all seemed so alone . . .

Isabel decided to help.
She planted flowers
in the paint pots.

She looked after stray animals.

And she helped to fix things up.

Then, day by day and week by week,
other people joined in, too.

And the more people came together . . .

the more they could all be seen.

Soon, Isabel wasn't just visible –
she was vibrant . . .

and so was her new home!

And that was how Isabel made something very special.
One of the hardest things that anyone can ever make . . .

Isabel had made a difference.

A Note from the Author

My earliest memory is of peering into a small cupboard in a caravan. I didn't know it at the time, but that caravan in rural South Shropshire was going to be my home for the next six years.

The caravan was old and the doors made a hollow, unsatisfying sound as you closed them. We had no television, we weren't connected to the mains electricity grid and we had gas lamps on the wall that you lit with a match. We got our drinking water from a spring in the garden, which was all well and good until the day we found a dead frog in it.

I shared a small room in the caravan with my older brother and I can still picture the ice glistening on the metal bedposts on cold winter mornings. In the depths of winter, it was literally freezing.

So, why did we live this way? In short, because we were poor.

However, despite our lack of money, despite the jumble sale clothes and hand-me-down shoes, there were two things that I had plenty of – love and books.

There was a mobile library service which parked up nearby. I would walk down the road clutching my pink library slips and be GIVEN as many books as I needed. But some people aren't as lucky as I was. Some people don't have access to that literary lifeline and the beauty and wonder of the countryside that I had free rein over as a child. Some people don't have love.

This is why I wanted to write Isabel's story. As of today, there are around four million children living in poverty in the UK[*]. That's over four million children who don't get enough food to eat, who are cold and tired, who don't have the equipment they need at school, who don't have the same chances and opportunities as everyone else. These children are often ignored, which is why I wanted to explore the idea of invisibility in this story.

Of course, poverty isn't the only way in which people get overlooked by society; there are many ways that the world has of saying, "you don't belong here".

I wanted to try to counter that. I wanted to say, "yes, you DO belong".

We all belong here.

Tom Percival
February 2020

* Child poverty facts and figures, The Children's Society website, UK